Anonymous

Catalogue of Books in the Legislative Council Library 1859

SALZWASSER VERLAG

Anonymous

Catalogue of Books in the Legislative Council Library 1859

Reprint of the original, first published in 1859.

1st Edition 2022 | ISBN: 978-3-37512-152-5

Verlag (Publisher): Salzwasser Verlag GmbH, Zeilweg 44, 60439 Frankfurt, Deutschland
Vertretungsberechtigt (Authorized to represent): E. Roepke, Zeilweg 44, 60439 Frankfurt, Deutschland
Druck (Print): Books on Demand GmbH, In de Tarpen 42, 22848 Norderstedt, Deutschland

CATALOGUE OF BOOKS

IN THE

LEGISLATIVE COUNCIL LIBRARY.

1859.

HALIFAX :

PRINTED BY JAMES BOWES AND SONS.

1859.

BOOKS PRESENTED BY HIS GRACE THE DUKE OF WELLINGTON, TO THE COLONY OF NOVA-SCOTIA.

[See Journals House of Assembly, 1838, App. 3.]

Acts of the Parliament of Scotland, from 2 to 11,   Vols. 10
Ancient Calendars and Inventories of His Majesty's
   Exchequer   3
Ancient Laws and Institutes of Wales   1
      "   "   England..   1
Calendarium Rotulorum Chartarum, et Inquisitionem
   ad Quad Damnum   1
Calendarium Rotulorum Patentium   1
Catalogue of Lansdowne Manuscripts in the British
   Museum   1
Doomsday Book.....   2
     "   Index and Supplement   2
Ducatus Lancastriae—Calendar to Pleadings   3
Eccerpta Rotulis Feineine in Turria Londenensi As-
   servatis—Hen. III., Reg...   2
Ecclesiasticus Taxatio—Cuca, A. D. 1291....   1
Ellis' Introduction and Indices to Doomsday Book.   2
Fines from 7th Richd. I. to 16th John   1
General Report of the Commissioners on Public
   Records, 1837...   1
Inquisitionum ad Capillam Domini Regis Retorna-
   tarum qua in Publicis Archives Scotia, ad huc
   servanter, Abbreviatio....   3
Inquisitionum in Officio Rotulorum Cancelariae Hi-
   berniae Asservatarum Repertorium   2
Inquisitionum Post Mortem Calendarium   4
Manuscripts in the Cottonian Library   1
    "   "   Harleian Collection...   4
Nonarum Inquisitiones in Curia Saccarii   1
Parliamentary Writs..   4

4

Placitorum Abbreviatio Temp.—Richard I., John, Henry III., Edward I., and Edward II....... Vols. 1
Placita de Quo Warranto Temp.—Edw. I., II., III. 1
Proceedings in Chancery—Queen Elizabeth 3
Proceedings and Ordinances of the Privy Councils of England—
    From 10th Richd. II. to 11th Hen. IV..... 1
    " 12th Hen. IV. to 10th Hen. V...... 1
    " 1st Hen. VI. to 7th Hen. VI........ 1
    " 8th Hen. VI. to 14th Hen. VI....... 1
    " 15th Hen. VI. to 21st Hen. VI...... 1
    " 22d Hen. VI. to 39th Hen. VI....... 1
    " 32d Hen. VIII. to 33d Hen. VIII.... 1
Record of Caernarvon 1
Registrum Magni Sigilli, 1306—1424.... 1
Reports of Commissioners on Public Records—1800 to 1819. 2
    Do. do. of Ireland—1810 to '15. 1
    " " " 1816 to '20. 1
    " " " 1821 to '25. 1
Rotulorum Patentium et Clausorum Cane'ae Hiberniae Calendarium. 1
Rotuli Literarum Clausorum 1
    " Patentium 1
    " Hundredorum 2
    " Scotiae in turri Londinensi et in domo Capitulari Westmonasteriensi.... 2
Rotulorum Originalium Abbreviatio.. 2
Rotuli Curiae Regis... 2
Rotulus Cancellarii 1
Rotuli Selecti ex Archives in Dom. Cap. West.... 1
Rotuli Normincae in Turri Londenensi 1
Rotulus Magnus Pipae 1
Rotuli de Oblates et Finibus 1
Rotuli Chartarum 1
Rymer's Foedera 6
Statutes of the Realm 9
    " " Chronological Index 1
    " " Alphabetical Index 1
    " " Charters of Liberties 1
Testa de Neville sive Liber Feodorum in Curia Saccarii 1
Valor Ecclesiasticus, Hen. VIII. 6

CATALOGUE.

Acts of the Parliament of Virginia, 1660 to 1748... Vols. 1
Addison's Complete Works 5
Alexander's Dictionary of Weights and Measures... 1
Alciphron's Epistles.. 1
Allen's Philosophy, Mechanics of Nature 1
Allison's Life of Marlborough....... 1
American Almanac from 1851 to '58. 8
Anacharsis' Travels in Greece 7
Annals of Congress from 1789 to '97. 6
Annual of Scientific Discovery, 1854 to '58, inclusive 5
Anthon's Dictionary, Greek and Roman Antiquities. 1
Anthon's English, Latin Lexicon.... 1
Anthon's, Charles, System of Ancient Geography .. 1
Appleton's Cyclopædia of Biography. 1
Aristotle's Treatise on Government.. 1
Arnold's History of Rome 1
Arnold's Miscellaneous Works...... 1
Artizan, the—1846 to '51 4
Art Journal, from 1839 to '57, inclusive.......... 16
Ascerbis' Travels.... 2
Assembly Journals of New York, 1850 to '55...... 9
Assembly Documents, 1850 to '55 ....; 41
   Senate Journals, 1850 to '55 6
   Senate Documents, 1850 to '55 17
Athenæum for 1857 2
Autobiography of Leigh Hunt 2
Aytoun's Lays of the Scottish Cavaliers 1

Bacon's Works .... Vols. 3
Bacon's Essays—Annotations by Whately 1
Badger's Description of the Nestorians and their
    Rituals 2
Bain's Wars 2
Baker's Livy 2
Bancroft's History of the United States... .....- 5
Barclay's Universal Dictionary.. 1
Barlow and Babbage's Cyclopedia of Manufactures
    and Machinery... 1
Barnard's National Education in Europe 1
Barnard's Isthmus of Tehuantepec 1
Baron's Life of Jenner 2
Barrow's Voyage to Arctic Regions 1
Barry Cornwall's Tales and Essays 2
Bartlett on Optics 1
Bartlett's Personal Narrative—Texas, Mexico, &c.. 2
Bartlett's Walks about Jerusalem 1
Bartlett's Forty Days in the Desert.. 1
Bassnett's Theory of Storms 1
Becker's Charicles.... 1
Beck's Medical Jurisprudence 2
Beckman's History of Inventions 2
Belcher's Voyage of the Samarang... 2
Bell's British Reptiles 1
Bell's Life of Canning..... 1
Beloe's Herodotus.... 1
Benger's, Miss, Memoirs of Mary Queen of Scots .. 2
Bentham's Works.... 11
Bewick's Select Fables.... 1
Bigsby's Shoe and Canoe 2
Blackwood's Magazine 10
Blain's Encyclopedia of Field Sports 1
Blain's Outlines of the Veterinary Art... 1
Blake's Biographical Dictionary 1
Bollingbrook's, Lord, Works 4
Book of British Ballads 1
Book-buyer's Manual 1
Booth and Morfit's Recent Improvements in Chemi-
    cal Arts 1
Borthwick's, J. D., Three Years in California 1
Boswell's, James, Letters 1

	Vols.
Boswell's Life of Samuel Johnson	2
Bourrienne's Life of Napoleon..	1
Boussingault's Rural Economy..	1
Boyer's French Dictionary	1
Brande's Manual of Chemistry..	2
Brand's Voyage to Peru	1
Brand's Encyclopedia of Science, Literature, &c...	1
Brewster's Magnetism	1
Brewster's More Worlds than One ..	1
British Essayists, viz : Mackintosh, Carlyle, Jeffrey, Talfourd and Stephen, Allison, Wilson, Smith, and Macaulay....	8
British Consul's Manual	1
British Almanac and Companion for 1858	1
British Eloquence	4
Brooke's Universal Gazetteer, London Edition	1
Brooke's Universal Gazetteer, American edition....	1
Brougham's, Lord, Analysis of Newton's Principia..	1
Broughton's Travels in Albania	2
Bruce's, James, Classic and Historic Portraits......	1
Buckingham's, Duke of. Memoirs of the Court of George II	4
Buckley's Translation of Euripides	2
Buffon's Natural History	2
Bunsen Chevalier's Life and Letters of Niebuhr....	1
Burke's, Right Hon. Edmund, Works....	2
Burke on Knightage ..	1
Burke's Royal Families of England, Scotland, and Wales..	2
Burke's Landed Gentry, Part 1.	1
Burke's Extinct Peerages of G. Britain and Ireland.	1
Burke's Romance of the Aristocracy	3
Burke's Peerage for 1854 and '58...	2
Burnett's Notes on N. W. Territory	1
Burton's Life and Correspondence of David Hume..	2
Burton's, John H., Criminal Trials in Scotland	2
Byrnes' Model Calculator	1
Byron's Complete Works..	1
Byron and Wallace's Voyage round the World	4

Calhoun's Works..... .... Vols. 4
Campbell's Poetical Works... 1
Campbell's, Lord, Lives of the Lord Chancellors ... 7
"   " Lives of the Chief Justices...... 2
Campbell's, George, India as it may be 1
Canada Directory—1857 and '58 1
Carey's Past, Present, and Future... 1
Carlyle's Dante's Inferno 1
Carlyle's Letters and Speeches of Oliver Cromwell... 2
Carlyle's French Revolution 2
Carlyle's, Goethe's, Wilhelm Meister 2
Carpenter's Human Physiology 1
Cassell's Family Paper 2
Catalogue of the New York State Library 1
    ..   Great Exhibition in London, 1851,
            royal 8vo. 3
    Another copy, large quarto. 8
    Catalogue of Exhibitors' Prospectuses 16
Catlin's North American Indians 2
Cathcart, Sir George, Correspondence of 1
Catalogue Parliamentary Library, Canada, 1857 and
    1858 2
Cavendish's Debates on the Quebec Bill 1
Channing's Works 6
Channing's Memoirs 3
Charlotte Elizabeth's Works.. 2
Chambers' Life of Robert Burns..... 4
Chatterton's Poetical Works 2
Chaucer's Poems 6
Chambers' Edinburgh Journal, first series... 12
    "   "   second series 20
    "   "   third series .. 9
    "   Cyclopedia of English Literature 2
    "   Information for the People...... 2
Chalmer's Daily Scripture Reading.. 3
    "   Institutes of Theology 2
    "   Sabbath Scripture Readings 2
    "   Sermons 1
    "   Prelictions on Butler's Analogy 1
    "   Correspondence... 1
    "   Memoirs of, by W. Hanna 4
    "   History Revolt of American Colonies,
        2 vols. in..................... 1

Chalmers' Introduction to the History of the Revolt
     of the American Colonies.......... Vols. 1
Chesney's Russo-Turkish Campaign 1
Churchill's Voyages 6
Clarendon's History of the Rebellion 2
Clarke's Concordance to Shakspeare 2
Classical Library, viz. :—
    Horace and Phedrus.... 2
    Potter's Aeschyles 1
    Cicero de Oratore 1
    Livy 5
    Pindar and Anacreon 1
    Cicero 3
    Sallust 1
    Sophocles 1
    Herodotus 3
    Cæsar 2
    Euripides 3
Cockburn's Life of Lord Jeffrey..... 1
    "   Memoirs of his own Times 1
Coleridge's Biographia Literaria 3
Colman's European Agriculture 2
    "   European Life and Manners 2
Colonial History of New York 3
Colton's, C., Public Economy 1
Comte's Positive Philosophy 2
Comic Blackstone 1
Confessions of Rosseau...... 1
Conquest of Canada... 2
Cooke's Voyage round the World 2
Coombe's System of Phrenology..... 1
Coombe's Animal Physiology 1
Cooper's Justinian.... 1
Courtenay's, T. P., Memoirs of Sir W. Temple 2
Cowper's Poetical Works.... 1
Crabbe's Synonymes 1
Cramer's History of Ancient Greece 3
Cresey's Cyclopedia of Civil Engineering 1
Cresswell's Theory of Mechanics 1
Crichton's, Andrew, History of Arabia and its People 1
Cultivator......... 9
Cumming's Five Years in the Interior of Africa 2

2

D'Abrante's Memoirs of Napoleon, his Court, &c.. Vols. 2
Dandy's Beautiful Islets of Britain 1
D'Arblay's, Madame, Diary and Letters 7
Darwin's Voyage of a Naturalist 1
Darling's Cyclopedia Bibliographia 1
Darly's Beaumont and Fletcher 2
Davy's Observations on the Ionian Isles and Malta.. 2
  " History of Holland and the Dutch... 3
  " El Gringo or New Mexico, its People, &c.. 1
Dawson's Acadian Geology... 1
Dawson's, J. H., Statistical History of Scotland.... 1
D'Aubigney's History of the Reformation 5
DeBoismont's History of Hallucinations 1
DeCustine's Russia as it is 1
De la Bech's Geological Observer 1
DeQuincy's Works, 10 vols., viz. :—
    The Cæsars 1
    Confessions of an English Opium Eater. 1
    Miscellaneous Essays 1
    Historical and Critical Essays 2
    Essays on Poems 1
    Literary Reminiscences.. 2
    Biographical Essays 1
    Life and Manners 1
DeTocqueville's Democracy in America 1
DeVere's, M. S., Comparative Philology.... 1
Dickens' Household Words 16
Dictionary, French Academy 2
Dixon's Life of William Penn 1
Documentary History of New York 4
Documents relating to the Colonial History of New
    York—vols. 1 to 9 (except vol. 2) 8
Dodd's Peerage of Great Britain and Ireland, 1858. 1
    " Parliamentary Companion, 1854 1
Donaldson's Treatise on Manures 1
Don Quixote, translated 1
Downing's Rural Essays..... 1
    " Horticulturist up to 1857. 11
Drinkwater's Siege of Gibraltar 1
Duncan's Cæsar and Sallust 1
Dunlop's History of Fiction.. 1
Dwyer's, Chas. P., Economic Cottage Builder 1

Eastwick's Autobiography of Lutfullah ...... Vols. 1
Eclectic Magazine, 1856 and '57 ......
Edinburgh Review up to 1857...... 6
Edinburgh Cabinet Library— 96
   Iceland, Greenland, &c. ......
   History of China 1
   Scandinavia, Ancient and Modern 3
   British India 2
   Italy and the Italian Islands.... 3
   Life of Henry the Eighth 3
   Discovery and Adventure in Africa 1
Edward's History of the West Indies 1
Ellets on the Mississippi and Ohio Rivers 6
Elliot's History of Roman Liberty 1
Ellis' Specimens of Early English Poetry 2
  " Treatise on Education.. 3
  " Aristotle's Treatise on Government 1
Emerson's English Traits.... 1
Emerson and Tenant's History of Modern Greece.. 1
Emmons' Philosophy of Popular Superstitions..... 2
Encyclopedia Metropolitana.. 1
Encyclopedia Americana 26
Ennemoser's History of Magic 14
Engineer for 1857.... 2
Euripides 2
3

Falkland's, Viscountess, Chow-Chow. ...... Vols. 2
Ferguson's Roman Republics. 1
Ferns of Great Britain and Ireland 1
Field's City Architecture 1
Fielding's Works 1
Field's Scrap Book 1
Folsom's Letters and Despatches of Fernando Cortez 1
Fontenell's Works 3
Forster's Life, &c., of Oliver Goldsmith 1
    "   Statesmen of the Commonwealth of England 1
Fortune's Tea Countries of China 2
Foster's Essays on Popular Ignorance...... 1
    "   Hand-book of European Literature 1
Flugel's German Dictionary.. 2
Francis', John, Chronicles and Characters of the
    Stock Exchange.. 1
Freedly's Treatise on Business 1
Fremont's Exploring Expedition through Oregon, &c. 1
Froissart's Chronicles. 2
Fry's, W. H., Treatise on Artificial Fish Breeding. 1
Fullon's Marvels of Science 1

Gan Eden, or Pictures of Cuba .... Vols. 1
Gerard, Jules, Adventures of. 1
Gerstaecker's Journey round the World 3
Gesner's Industrial Resources of Nova Scotia 1
Gifford's Ben Johnson 1
.. Life of Pitt 3
Gillies' History of Ancient Greece... 1
Gleig's Memoirs of Warren Hastings 3
Goodrich's Pictorial History of America 1
.. History of all Nations 2
Goethe's Faust 1
Goldsmith's Animated Nature 2
.. Miscellaneous Works 4
Golownin's Japan and the Japanese 2
Gordon's History of the Greek Revolution 2
Gore's Rose-fancier's Manual 1
Graham's Colonial History of the United States.... 2
Gray's Works 5
Grandville's Fables 1
Greeley's Art and Industry of the Crystal Palace 1
Gregg's Commerce of the Prairies 2
Gregory's Mathematics 1
Gregory's, Dr., Animal Magnetism 1
Grey's, Earl, Colonial Policy. 2
Grote's History of Greece 12
Grove's Greek and English Dictionary 1
Guizot's Corneille and his Times.... 1
.. Memoirs of Sir Robert Peel 1
.. History of Civilization...... 4
.. History of Oliver Cromwell 2
.. Shakspeare and his Times... 1
Gurouski's Russia as it is.... 1
Gurwood's General Orders of Wellington, 2d edition 1
Gwilt's Cyclopedia of Architecture 1

Hackle's Hints on Angling .... Vols. 1
Hale's, S. J., Dictionary of Poetical Quotations 1
Haliburton's Yankee Stories 1
    "   History of Nova Scotia 2
    "   Rule and Misrule...... 1
Hallam's Works 4
Hall's, Mrs. S. C., Sketches of Irish Character..... 1
Hamilton's, Sir W., Philosophy 1
Hampton's Polybius 2
Hand-book of Oil Painting... 1
Hansard's Parliamentary Debates 75
Hannay's Satire and Satirists. 1
Harper's Magazine 15
    "   Universal Gazetteer. 1
    "   General History for Schools 1
Hart's Army List for 1858... 1
Hasheesh Eater, The.. 1
Hatsel's Precedents 4
Haupt on Bridge Construction...... 1
Hawk's Peruvian Antiquities. 1
Hawker on Shooting.. 1
Hays' Peninsular War 1
Hayden's Dictionary of Dates 1
    "   Lectures on Painting 2
Hazlitt's Works...... 11
Head's, Sir E., Hand-book of Spanish Painting.... 1
Herschel's Outlines of Astronomy 1
Herbert's Prometheus and Agamemnon 1
Hildreth's History of the United States, 1st and 2d
    series.. 6
Hildreth's Theory of Politics 1
Hills of the Shatemuc 1
Hitchcock's Geology of the Globe 1
Hogarth's Works 1
    "   (a second copy)... 2
Hogg's History f the Microscope 1
Holland's, Lady, Memoirs of Sydney Smith ... 2
Holmes' Views in the Great Metropolis 1
Holyoake's Hints on Public Speaking 1
Household of Sir Thomas Moore 1
Huc's Christianity in China 2
Hughes' Scripture Geography... 1

16   Vols. 1

Illustrated Times..... .... Vols. 5
Illustrated Description of New York Crystal Palace, 1
Illustrated London Library, 8 vols., viz. :
    The Colonies of Australia...... 1
    Our Iron Roads 1
    Life of Wellington 2
    The French in Algeria 1
    English Forests and Forest Trees 1
    The Three Presidencies of India 1
    Lares and Penates 1
Imperial Gazetteer 1
Inquire Within 1
Irving's Works (complete)... 15
    " Knickerbocker's History of New York..... 1

3

18

Jackson's Geology of New Hampshire ...... Vols. 1

6

James' Naval History 1

"   Fables of Æsop 2

"   G. P. R., Life of Henry the Fourth.. 1

Jamieson's Treatise on Mechanics ... 1

Jenkins', J. S., United States' Exploring Expeditions 1

Johnston's Lectures on Agricultural Chemistry..... 1

Johnston's, A. K., Physical Atlas 1

"   National Atlas 2

Johnson's Farmers' and Planters' Cyclopedia, 1

Johnstone's Travels in Abyssinia.... 21

Johnson's British Poets 1

Iominis' Art of War.. 1

Jones' Treatise on the Electric Telegraph... 1

"   History of Ancient America .. ..

Journals of House of Assembly of Nova Scotia, from 29

1793 to 1857 ....

Journals of Legislative Council of Nova Scotia, from 21

1836 to '57 ....

Journals of House of Assembly of Newfoundland, 2

1840 and '46 2

"   Council of Newfoundland, 1849 and '50,

"   Provincial Congress of New York, 1775 2

to 1777 ....

"   Legislative Assembly of Canada, 1852 2

and '53 9

Appendix to ditto ....

Journals of Legislative Assembly of Canada. 1854 2

and '55 14

Appendix to ditto 1

Index to Journal and Appendix 1

Journals of Legislative Assembly of Canada, 1856.. 6

Appendix to ditto 1

Journals of Legislative Assembly of Canada, 1857.. 1

Appendix to ditto, No. 2 2

Journals of Legislative Assembly of Canada, 1858.. 1

Journals of Legislative Council, 1854 and '55 14

Sessional Papers, 1854 and '55 1

Journals of Legislative Council, 1856 6

Sessional Papers, 1856 ....

Journals of House of Assembly of New Brunswick, 17

from 1837 to '57, except '47, '51, '52,

Journals of Legislative Council of New Brunswick,Vols. 24
          from 1786 to 1857, except for 1831,
          '32, '33, 34, '38 and '46 ......

Journals of House of Assembly of P. E. Island from
          1839 to '57, except '40, '41, '42, '47,
          and '54 14

Journals of Legislative Council of P. E. Island from
          1836 to '52, except '37, '43, '44, '45,
          and '48 12

Journals of Legislative Council of Canada, 1857.... 1

Sessional Papers accompanying ditto... 10

       "   being plans of the Lakes and
              Rivers from Lake Huron to
              the River Ottawa 1

       "   being maps of Canals, connect-
              ed with Report of Commis-
              sioners of Crown Lands.... 1

Journals of the House of Lords, from the 1st Henry
          VIII., 1509, to 18th Victoria, 1854,
          except vol. 85 ; total number of vols.
          on hand, including the 86th........ 85

General Index to ditto for vols. 1 to 10....... 1
     "   "   11 to 19....... 1
     "   "   20 to 35....... 1
     "   "   36 to 52....... 1

Rolls of Parliament to supply deficiencies in the
          Lords' Journals 7

General Index to ditto from 1278 to 1503 1

Calendar of the Lords' Journals, 1509 to 1808, 1
       "   "   1808 to 1826, 1

Journals of the House of Commons from 1st Edward
          VI., 1547, to 21st Vic., 1857, except
          16th vol. 112

General Index to ditto for vols. 1 to 7...... 1
     "   "   8 to 11...... 1
     "   "   12 to 17...... 1
     "   "   18 to 35...... 1
     "   "   35 to 55...... 1
     "   "   56 to 75...... 1

Kayes' History of the East India Company ...... Vols. 1

" Portraits 4

" History of the War in Afghanistan 2

Kingsley's, Charles, Two Years Ago 1

King's Geology and Religion 1

Kitto's Cyclopedia of Biblical Literature.... 1

Knight's Cyclopedia of London 1

" Half Hours with the Best Authors. 4

(A second copy).... 2

" Knowledge is Power 1

Knox's Manual of Artistic Anatomy.. 1

Koran of Mahomet 1

Krotel's, Rev. G. F., Life of Melancthon 1

Lamartine's History of the Girondists ...... Vols. 3
"   Memoirs of Celebrated Characters   3
"   Restoration of Monarchy in France.... 4
Land we Live in   2
Lardner's Railway Economy   1
Las Casas' Memoirs of Napoleon   4
Latham's English Grammar   1
Law Privileges and Usages of Parliament...   1
Laws of P. E. Island, 1773 to 1834..   1
"   1837, '43, '47, '48 and '52   5
Laws of New York from 1691 to 1773   1
"   1850, '51, '52, '54 & '55   5
Laws of Nova Scotia from 1758 to 1826....   3
"   "   1837 to 1857   20
    Revised Statutes of Nova Scotia   1
    Private and Local Acts of Nova Scotia 1
Laws of N. Brunswick from 1836 to '57, except '47, 19
Layard's Nineveh and its Remains...   2
"   Second Expedition to Nineveh   1
Lester's Life and Voyages of Americanus Vespacius, 1
Leslie's, Sir John, Polar Seas and Regions 1
Leuchar's Treatise on Hot Houses   1
Lewes', G. H., Life and Works of Goethe 2
Lewis', G. C., Method of Reasoning in Politics 2
Liddell and Scott's Greek and English Lexicon 1
Lingard's History of England.   13
Liebig's Complete Works on Chemistry   1
Lippincott's Pronouncing Gazetteer of the World 1
Lippincott and Grambos' Gazetteer of the U. States, 1
Livingston's Missionary Travels in South Africa.... 1
Lodge's Illustrations of British History.....   3
"   Portraits.....   8
London Quarterly Review up to 1857......   90
Long and Potter's America and West Indies 1
Long's France and its Revolutions   1
Lower's Essays on English Surnames   1
Low's Domesticated Animals.   1
Lowy's History of Chivalry and Ancient Armor 1

Mackay's Western World .... Vols. 2
Mackintosh's Life of Sir J. Mackintosh..... 2
MacGregor's Commercial Statistics... 5
MacCulloch's Commercial Dictionary, edition of 1843 2
    "   "   " 1850 1
Macaulay's History of England...... 4
Macfarlane's History of Japan 1
Macilwain's Memoirs of Abernethy 1
Machiavelia's History of the Florentines.... 1
Macaulay's Speeches.. 2
McIain's Costumes of the Clans, parts 1 to 8,
McKenzie's Six Years in Delhi 1
McFarlane's History of British India 1
MacGeoghegan's History of Ireland.. 1
Madan's Translation of Juvenal 2
Magnetic and Meteorological Observations 8
Magazine of Art 4
Mahon's History of England 2
Mahon's History of England (a second copy) 7
Mayhew's Treatise on Horse's Mouth 1
Malte-Brun's Geography..... 1
Martineau's, Harriet, History of England during the
    Peace.. 2
Martin's History of the British Colonies 1
    "   " Eastern India 3
Markham's, C. R., Cusco and Lima.. 1
Massinger's Plays 1
Maunder's Scientific and Literary Treasury 1
    " Treasury of Natural History..... 1
Maury's Physical Geography of the Sea 1
Mechanics' Magazine 6
Medlock's Book of Nature 1
Mensell's History of Literature 3
Merivale's History of the Romans under the Empire, 3
Meteorology of New York, 1826 to 1850 ... 1
Mexican War (illustrated) 1
Michelet's History of France.. 2
    " French Revolution 1
Middleton's Life and Letters of Cicero 1
Milton's Works...... 8
Miller's, Hugh, Schools and Schoolfellows... 1
    " Testimony of the Rocks 1

Miller's, Hugh, Old Red Sandstone.. ...... Vols. 1
"   First Impressions of England   1
"   Footprints of the Creator   1
"   Geology of the Bass Rock...   1
Mills' Political Economy   2
Milne's, Rev. W. C., Life in China   1
Mills and Wilson's History of British India 9
Mirror of Parliament from 1828 to 1837. ...   36
     "   "   1837-8 to 1841   25
Mitford's History of Greece   8
Mitchell's Planetary and Stellar Worlds   1
"   Orbs of Heaven   1
Modern Atlas   1
Moore's Life of Sheridan.....   2
Montaign's Works....   1
Monstrelet's Chronicles......   2
Montalembert's Political Future of England   1
Motley's History of the Rise of the Dutch Republic, 3
          (Another copy, cloth)..   3
Muller's Physics and Meteorology   1
Munro's History of New Brunswick, Nova Scotia,
     and P. E. Island   1
Murphy's Works of Tacitus   1
Murray's Tour on the Thames   1
Musee Royale   2

Napier's History of the Peninsular War.... Vols. 1
Napoleon Dynasty....   1
Napoleon's Correspondence with King Joseph · 2
National Gallery of Pictures 2
Natural History of New York.   17
Naturalist's Library...   40
Naunton's Court of Queen Elizabeth 1
Newman and Barretti's Spanish Dictionary 1
Newman's, F. W., Defence of the Eclipse of Faith. 1
New York State Library — Catalogue of General
      Library......   1
    Do.   do.   do.   Law Library. 1
Nichols' Architecture of the Heavens   1
Nicholson's Mechanics' Companion 1
Niebuhr's Ancient History...   3
Nocte's Ambrosiana...   5
Norris' Hand-book of Locomotives and Machinery.. 1
Northern Coasts of America, Description of 1
North British Review from 1852 to '57..... 6
Nott and Gliddon's Types of Mankind   1
Notices of Public Libraries in the United States 1
Notes on the Early History of Babylon (pamphlet). 1
Nova Scotia Debates, 1856 1

4

Ockley's History of the Saracens .... Vols. 1
O'Kelly's History of Ireland..   1
Olmstead's Journey through Texas...   1
      "   Journey through the Slave States.   1
Oliphant's Russian Shores of the Black Sea   1
O'Meara's Napoleon in Exile.   2
Oscanyan's Sultan and his People   1
Overman's Practical Mineralogy   1
Overland Route, Gleanings on the...   1
Owen's British Fossil Mammals   1
      "   Geological Survey   1

Page's Theory of Teaching .... Vols. 1
Paley's Works. 1
Pardoe's Louis XIV.. 2
Parkyn's Life in Abyssinia... 2
Parishe's History of Buenos Ayres... 1
Parliamentary Papers, viz :
    Reports on Common Law...... 4
    Chancery Practice 2
    Papers on Canada 4
    Ecclesiastical Courts 1
    Criminal Laws... 1
    Real Property 2
    Law Commissioners of Scotland. 1
    Aborigines of British Settlements..... 1
    Tables of the United Kingdom.. 1
    Stockale V. S. Hansard.. 1
    Papers on Canada, 2d sett 3
Patent Office Reports from 1845-6 to '56... 19
Peel, Sir Robert, Memoirs of 2
Peel's, Sir Robert, Speeches.. 4
Percy's Relics of Old English Romance 1
    "   Anecdotes 1
    "   Relics of Ancient English Poetry 3
Percival's Anatomy of the Horse 1
    "   Veterinarian 3
    "   Disorders and Lamenesses of Horses 2
Perley's Report on the Fisheries of New Brunswick 1
Perry's Expedition to Japan.. 1
Peirce's Treatise on Sound 1
Pfeiffer's Visit to the Holy Land 1
    "   Visit to Iceland 1
Phillips' Mineralogy 1
    "   Metallurgy... 1
Pickering's Races of Man.... 1
Pictures from the Battle Fields 1
Piggott's Treatise on Copper Mining 1
Pilkington's Dictionary of Painters 1
Plato's Works. 4
Plough, Loom and Anvil 6
Poole's Index of Periodical Literature...... 1
Porter's Five Years in Damascus.... 2
Post Office Directory, London, 1841 1

Potter's History of Charnwood Forest ...... Vols. 1
Precedents and Proceedings of the House of Com-
    mons 4
Prescott's Conquest of Peru 2
    " Conquest of Mexico 3
    " Ferdinand and Isabella 3
Prime's Travels in Europe 2
    " Boat Life in Egypt and Nubia 1
Prior's Life of Burke 2
Proceedings in Chancery (Reign of Queen Elizabeth) 3
Provincial, The 2
Public General Acts from 7th William IV. to 4th
    Victoria 4
Public General Acts from 9th to 11th Victoria..... 2
    " " 13th to 15th Victoria 2
    " " 17th to 21st Victoria, up to
            1857... 5
Pugin's Gothic Architecture.. 2
Putnam's Universal Biography...... 1
    " Hand-book of Useful Arts 1
    " World's Progress 1
    " Hand-book of Literature and Fine Arts .. 1

Quintus Curtius...... .... Vols. 2

Rambler and Idler.... .... Vols. 1
Ranke's History of Prussia... 3
" History of the Popes 2
Reed's Memoirs of Wordsworth 2
Redfield's, J. W., Comparative Physiognomy...... 1
" Men of the Time. 1
Reid's Intellectual Powers of Man... 1
Report on the United States Coast Survey of 1853. 1
Report of Board of Trade and Navigation of Canada
     for 1857...... 1
Report on Public Accounts of Canada for 1857 1
Revised Statutes of Massachusetts, 1836 1
" Supplement to ditto, 1836 to '44... 1
Richardson's Arctic Expedition 1
Ritter's History of Ancient Philosophy..... 4
Robertson's Gibraltar and Peninsular 1
Robertson's Works 9
Rogers' Poetical Works 1
" Table Talk 1
Roget's Animal and Vegetable Physiology 2
" Thesaurus, English Words 1
Rollin's Ancient History 4
Romilly, Sir Samuel, Life of 2
Roscoe's Life of Leo X...... 4
Ross' Arctic Expedition 1
" Voyage to Baffin's Bay. 1
" Second Voyage to Arctic Regions 1
Rousseau's Confessions...... 1
Rules and Orders of House of Representatives of
     Massachusetts 1
Russell's Modern Europe 3
Russell's, Lord John, Memoirs of C. J. Fox. 4
Russell's Letters on the War in the Crimea 2
Russell's, Lord John, Memoirs of Thomas Moore, 4
Russell's Memoirs of Fox 2
Ruskin's Seven Lamps of Architecture 1

Sabine's American Loyalists...   Vols. 1
Schoolcraft's History of North American Indians...   3
Schlosser's History of the Eighteenth Century,   8
Schroeder's Maxims of Washington..   1
Schlegel's Lectures on Dramatic History....   1
Scrope's, G. P., Life of Lord Sydenham   1
Scott's, Sir W., Waverly Novels   27
Scott's Poetical Works   1
Seaman's Progress of Nations.   1
Seneca's Morals......   1
Shea's, J. G., Discovery and Exploration on the Mis-
  sissippi   1
Shakspeare's Complete Works   8
Shakspearian Society's Works   19
Shelly's Poetical Works   1
Shiel's Sketches of the Irish Bar   2
Silliman's Visit to Europe....   2
Skinner's Treatise on Milch Cows ...   1
Slick's Wise Saws   1
    "   Nature and Human Nature...   1
Smee on Instinct and Reason.   1
Smiles' Life of George Stephenson...   1
Smith's Thucydides   1
    "   Lectures on Modern History   1
    "   Natural History of the Human Species....   1
    "   Dictionary of Arts, Sciences, and Manu-
          factures...   2
    "   Dictionary of Greek and Roman Biography
          and Mythology   3
    "   Longinus   1
    "   Mediterranean   1
    "   History of Virginia ..   1
    "   Wealth of Nations   1
    "   Canada, Past, Present and Future..   2
Smithsonian Contributions to Knowledge   9
Smithsonian Reports for 1855–6   2
Southgate's Travels in Armenia.....   2
Spectator......   1
    (A second copy)..   1
Standing Orders of the House of Lords, 2 copies, '25   2
    "   "   House of Lords and Com-
                    mons, 1857   1

Spooner's Dictionary of Painters, Engravers, &c ... Vols. 1
Statutes of the Realm 10
    Chronological Index to ditto.... 1
    Alphabetical Index to ditto 1
Statutes at Large of Great Britain... 12
   " of Upper Canada, Revised, from 1792 to
        1840, vol. 1 Public Acts 1
   " of Upper Canada, Local and Private Acts,
        vol. 2.. 1
   " of Lower Canada, Revised, with tables, 1
   " of United Canada, 1841, '42 and '43...... 1
   " " 1844 and '45.... 1
   " " 1850 1
   " " 1851 1
   " " 1852 and '53, part 1;
             1854 and '55, part 1, 2
   " " 1856, '57 and '58...... 3
State Papers during the reign of Henry VIII. 5
Steinmetzs' History of the Jesuits 2
Stephens' Farmer's Guide.... 2
Stephens on the English Constitution 2
Stephens' Travels in Egypt and the Holy Land, 1
Stevenson on Marine Surveying, &c. 1
Stewart's Moral and Active Powers of Man.. 1
Stiles', W. H., Austria in 1848–9... 2
Stocqueler's Life of Wellington 1
     " History of India 1
Stowe's. Mrs., Sunny Memories of Foreign Lands, 2
Stryker's American Register 2
Strickland's, Miss, Queens of England...... 12
     " Queens of Scotland 6
Stuart's Dictionary of Architecture 2
     " Mail Steamers of the United States 1
     " Dry Docks of the United Sttates... 1
     " Philosophy of the Human Mind 1
St. Pierre's Works 2
Swift's Works 2
Swinburne's Letters from the Court of France, &c. 2

Tasso's Jerusalem Delivered .... Vols. 1
Tattler and Guardian 1
  (A second copy).. 1
Taylor's Memoirs of the House of Orleans... 2
  " Statistics of Coal 1
  " Proclus 2
Thaer's Principles of Agriculture.... 1
Thackeray's Pendennis...... 2
Thiers' History of the French Revolution 1
  " History of the French Consulate and the
         Empire.... 1
Thomas' Asmodeus 1
Thomson's Wanderings among Wild Flowers...... 1
  " Travels in Western Himalaya and Tibet. 1
Ticknor's History of Spanish Literature.. 3
Townsend's, W. C., Modern State Trials 2
      " Lives of twelve Eminent Judges 2
Train's Young American Abroad 1
Transactions of the American Institute 1
     " New York State Agricultural
         Society 2
Trench's Lessons in Proverbs 1
Turner's Architecture of the Middle Ages 1
Twelve Cæsars, Lives of the 2
Twiss' Life of Lord Eldon 2
Tytler's Life of Henry VIII. 1
  " Universal History 2
  " History of Scotland 7

5

Wade's British History .... Vols. 1
   " England's Greatness. 1
Walker's Analysis of Beauty 1
   " Rhyming Dictionary 1
   " Expedition to Nicaragua.. 1
Walpole's Letters to George Montague..... 3
   " Complete Works 5
   " Memoirs of the Reign of George III. 4
   " Letters to Sir Horace Mann 4
Walton and Cotton's Angler. 1
Warburton's Conquest of Canada.... 2
Warton's History of English Poetry 3
Waterston's Cyclopedia of Commerce 1
Webster's, Daniel, Works.... 6
   " Dictionary of the English Language, 1
   " Diplomatic and Official Papers 1
Wellington's Speeches in Parliament 2
Well's Antiquities of Spain 1
Welsh's Military Reminiscences 2
Westminster Review, 1852 to '57 6
Whateley's Elements of Logic...... 1
Wheeler's Homes for the People 1
Wheelright's Comedies of Aristophanes 2
Whewell's Philosophy of Inductive Sciences, 2
   " History of Inductive Sciences ... 3
Whiston's Works of Josephus...... 1
Whitney's Metallic Wealth of the United States, 1
Wines' Laws of the Ancient Hebrews...... 1
Winterbotham's History of America. 4
Wild Flowers of Nova Scotia (4 parts).....
Wilkes', Chas., United States Exploring Expedition, 5
Wilkinson's Ancient Egyptians..... 2
Wilson's American Ornithology 1
Wittick's Curiosities of Physical Geography 1
Wordsworth's Pictorial Greece 1
World of Art and Industry, illustrated 1
Wright's Sketches of Sorcery and Magic.... 1
Wycherly and Congreve's Dramas... 1